It's a Baby-Sitter's Nightmare...

"Gimme half the money my parents are paying you and maybe I'll be your friend."

D.J. laughed. Even though it wasn't very funny. This kid was a spoiled little monster. "No way, Brian. I'm saving up to buy my own phone. So, would you like to play a nice quiet game? Or would you like to go right to sleep?" Hint-hint.

Brian leapt up onto the back of the couch and assumed a karate pose. "I'm the Black Ninja Warrior Prince. And you're the Evil Lord Carnux from Dimension Zilch. Kneel before me or I'll Ninjitsu you."

He started chopping the air with his hands.

D.J. backed off, trying to stay cool. "I'm not kneeling before you, Brian."

"Wanna bet?" He grabbed a vase off the coffee table. A very expensive-looking vase. "Do what I say or I'll smash this and say you did it."

Published by
Dell Publishing by arrangement with Parachute Press, Inc.

Dell Publishing
a Division of
Bantam Doubleday Dell Publishing Group, Inc.
666 Fifth Avenue
New York, NY 10103

ISBN: 044-0-40468-1
Printed in the United States of America
September 1990
10 9 8 7 6 5 4 3 2 1

FULL HOUSE

SAME TO YOU, DUCK FACE

by Bonnie Worth

Based on the series **FULL HOUSE** created by
Jeff Franklin

and on episodes written by:
Lenny Ripps
Jeff Franklin
Shari Scharfer & Julie Strassman

A PARACHUTE PRESS BOOK

FULL HOUSE

SAME TO YOU, DUCK FACE

ONE

D. J. Tanner stood before the full-length mirror in her bedroom arranging her hair, one long, honey-gold strand at a time.

She stood back to study the effect. Her little sister Stephanie, seven going on thirty-eight, looked on solemnly. She held a king-size can of hair spray in her hand. A second can stood on the dresser.

"D. J.," Stephanie said, "if it's not right by now, put on a hat."

"Stephanie," her big sister explained carefully, "today is my first day of junior high school. I want to look perfect."

Making one last careful placement, she cried, "There! Quick! Spray!"

At that, the sisters emptied the contents of both cans onto D. J.'s perfect head.

Coughing and sputtering, Stephanie emerged from the perfumed fog. She reached out and poked D. J.'s hair. Cement helmet was more like it.

"Very natural," she commented sarcastically. "Now, do you mind if I pay a little attention to my own preparations? Which barrettes should I wear?" she wondered aloud. "The lime-green poodles? Or the magenta bunny rabbits. Talk about your major life decisions!"

D. J. plucked at her blouse. She tugged at the waistband of her pants. Were they too baggy? Was the color right? She had changed three times already—from pants to a skirt and back into pants again. Suddenly she hated everything in her closet. But this would just have to do.

"Well!" she cried, sighing. "At last I'm finally going to a school that doesn't have a sandbox."

"How can you be so happy?" Stephanie frowned, pulling on her knee socks. "This is the first time we won't be in the same school. Aren't you gonna miss me like crazy?"

"Stef, try to understand. You are a child. I am a young adult. And starting today, we live in different worlds."

Stephanie eyed the mess on D.J.'s side of the room that had spilled over onto her own. "We sure don't live in different *rooms*."

D. J. rolled her eyes. "Please don't remind me."

Stephanie came over to the mirror. She checked to make sure the magenta bunnies were firmly fixed in her curly blond hair. Then she threw a friendly arm around her sister.

"Come on, Deej. Stay at my school. I need my big sister to stick up for me. What if some kid calls me a lameoid zombie dog?"

D. J. shrugged and flashed her famous half grin. "I don't know. Bite 'em, I guess. Look, I never had a big sister to stick up for me. I did fine and so will you."

Stephanie wasn't so sure. "By the time I get to junior high, you'll be in high school. When I get to high school, you'll be in college. When I get to college, you'll be working at McDonald's."

D. J. sighed. "I'm going to miss these little chats."

TWO

Downstairs in the Tanner house, the usual circus was in progress. The girls' father, Danny Tanner, was in the kitchen fixing the bag lunches. His youngest daughter, the two-and-a-half-year-old imp, Michelle, was "helping" him.

In the living room, the girls' cute young Uncle Jesse was trying to listen in on a telephone conversation. His best buddy and business partner, Joey, was speaking with one of their new advertising clients. The partners worked at home—home meaning the Tanner house. How had this come about?

About two years ago, not long after Danny's wife, the girls' mother, had been killed in a car accident, Jesse and Joey had been looking for an apartment. Moving in with the Tanners had been just a temporary arrangement. Jesse stayed in the guest room upstairs. Joey stayed in the finished basement. It was a bit crowded. But somehow it worked. The two guys helped Danny with the three girls. They had discovered that one dad per girl was just what was needed. Sometimes, in fact, it felt as if they could use *another* pair of hands. But there was no more room. It was a full house. And most of the time, a pretty happy one, too.

The doorbell rang. Jesse stopped his eavesdropping to answer it. What a nice surprise! It was Rebecca. Rebecca was the co-host of Danny Tanner's local talk show. And Jesse's steady girlfriend.

They kissed as D.J.'s best friend, Kimmy, ducked past them through the open door.

"This early!" she cracked. "I hope you brushed."

"Character" was the best way to describe Kimberly Gibbler.

Jesse turned from Rebecca. "Kimmy, I've got a wild idea. How about if this year, D.J. picks *you* up for school."

"No can do," Kimmy said. She waved to D.J. as she came downstairs. "My dad eats breakfast in his underwear."

Danny Tanner came in from the kitchen. "Here's your lunch." He handed the neatly rolled paper bag to D.J. Danny Tanner was Mr. Neatness himself.

Kimmy was not impressed. "Mr. Tanner, get with the program," she told him. "In junior high, the cool kids buy their lunch. If you want to be a good dad, give her a bag of cash."

Danny took out his wallet. "Here, honey,

buy some lunch and," he added sweetly, "make some new friends."

Rebecca could tell the girls were pretty nervous. "Don't worry," she told them. "You guys are going to have a great time. Junior high was when I got my first boyfriend, my first slow dance, my first real kiss—"

Danny shot her a warning look.

"And then I woke up and it was all a dream!" Rebecca finished innocently.

But the girls weren't fooled. They grinned. They knew junior high was the start of a whole new life. D.J. kissed her dad good-bye. She kissed her Uncle Jesse. She waved to Joey, who was still on the phone.

"Bye, everybody," she called. "See you later."

"Wait for me!" Michelle came zooming in from the kitchen. "I go, too!"

Joey hung up the phone with one hand. He grabbed Michelle by the seat of her trapdoor jammies with the other. "Hold on you little Sesame Streaker. You don't start nursery school until next year."

"Here, Michelle." D.J. handed her the brown bag. "Practice with a real school lunch." Then she and Kimmy headed out for the bus.

Michelle peered into the bag. "No cookies?"

Next came Stephanie, trudging down the stairs.

"Well, I'm going now," she said gloomily. "The only Tanner left in my whole school."

"Stef—" Danny began.

"No!" Stephanie held up a noble hand. "Really, it's a beautiful thing."

"Stef," he went on, "I know you're a little scared. But trust me, everything is going to work out just fine."

"So I guess I shouldn't even bother with the phony cough."

"No."

Stephanie nodded. Resigned to her fate,

9

she turned to the door. "Here I go. The only Tanner."

And with a deep breath, she walked bravely out the door. On her way to the first day of second grade.

THREE

The junior high school cafeteria was a zoo that morning. Everybody in the school was there to register for class. D.J. reeled off to the S to Z line, clutching her schedule.

She looked around her in total awe. Everybody looked so big. All the girls wore makeup. And such hot outfits! A clique of heavily madeup, especially hot-looking eighth-grade girls passed D.J. One of them bumped into her. *Maybe* it was an accident. But somehow D.J. didn't think so.

"Look out, dweeb," one of the girls said, tossing her blond hair. The letters on the gold necklace she wore said "Colleen."

D.J. backed out of her way. She stammered apologies.

Colleen said to her friends, "These new kids are so *tiny*—they're infants."

Laughing cruelly, they moved off.

D.J. shriveled inside. Just as she was about to dry up and blow away, she saw a sight for sore eyes. "Kimmy!" she shouted above the din.

"D.J.!"

They ran to each other and latched on for dear life.

"Don't ever leave my side again," D.J. said.

Just then a boy passed them. Was that a real mustache growing on his upper lip?

"Can you *believe* these people?" Kimmy marveled. "They're like totally...*mature!*"

Over in the far corner a boy and a girl were not just kissing. They were really *smooching*! "Where *are* we?" D.J. wondered aloud. "Young and the Restless Junior High?"

"Let me see your schedule." Kimmy grabbed it. Her bony shoulders sagged. "We only have one class together. Sixth-period Spanish."

"Figures," D.J. said dully. "The only time we're together we can't speak English."

Just then a girl came over to them. "D.J., Gibbler," she said casually. "Hi."

The girls looked hard at her. She seemed to know them. But did they know her? She looked like something out of a radical rock video. Skintight black-leather skirt. Real stockings. High heels. And about ninety tons of makeup.

"Do we know you?" D.J. asked uneasily.

"Duh," she said. "We only went to school together for the last six years. Kathy Santoni?"

"Kathy Santoni?" the girls chimed. Skinny little Kathy Santoni? Now she had more curves than a mountain road.

"You grew up," Kimmy said, gulping.

"Big time," D.J. agreed.

"Pretty intense summer," Kathy drawled. She looked around at the crowd as she spoke to them. "Okay, now here's what I found out so far. All the cute guys take metal shop and everyone hangs out after school on the football field."

"Everyone?" Kimmy brightened.

Kathy looked both girls up and down. Scrubbed faces. Goody-goody outfits. "Well, maybe not *everyone*. See you." And she wiggled off in her tight leather skirt, black stockings, and ultra-high heels.

Just then the bell rang. It was time for classes. The guy with the mustache passed again. Colleen and the Snobs passed too, giggling. Probably about them.

"Well," Kimmy said gloomily. "Guess we gotta go."

"I don't know," D.J. said in a small voice. "I think I'll go back to sixth grade. I mean, Stephanie really needs me."

FOUR

At lunch that day D.J. came off the food line carrying her tray and looked around the crowded, noisy room. She was looking for a friendly face. Or just a familiar one. She didn't see either.

But what was this? Someone was waving. At her! And it was those snobby eighth-grade girls. They wanted her to join their table! Maybe they weren't so snobby, after all.

She crossed over to them.

"Thanks," she said, "my name's—"

"Not you, dweeb," said a voice behind her.

She turned and saw Colleen, the girl who had bumped into her accidentally-on-purpose earlier today. The others had been signaling her, not D.J. "Figures," she thought.

Blushing to the tips of her ears, D.J. backed off. Colleen said to her friends, "Another year of Mrs. Agbabian on cafeteria duty. Good way to lose your lunch."

D.J. felt someone tap her on the shoulder. She turned. It was none other than Agbabian herself. And she did not look happy.

"Find a seat and get settled," she said grouchily.

D.J. found herself staring at the woman. No, it couldn't be! It was impossible. *But it was*. Agbabian was dressed in an outfit *just like* the one D.J. was wearing.

The slick clique noticed it, too. They started laughing. The laughter spread from table to table. Before long, the entire cafeteria was laughing. At D.J. Tanner. She would never, ever be able to live this down.

She wanted to curl up and die.

Mrs. Agbabian blew a whistle.

"That will be enough of that!" she shouted. Turning to D.J., she said, "That's a very smart outfit, young lady. Now, be seated."

More laughter. D.J. boiled with embarrassment as she turned and walked off. But where did she think she was going to sit? Everyone was staring at her. No one was offering her a seat. Tray and all, she walked right into the only place she could hide—the telephone booth. She swung the door shut behind her. With a little luck, she could spend the rest of her life in here.

She sneaked a look over her shoulder. People were still looking at her. Didn't they have anything better to do with their lunch hour? They wanted to see what she was going to do, standing in the phone booth, lunch tray and all. She knew what she wanted to do. She wanted to phone Uncle Jesse and Joey and tell them to pick her up right away. She would go home and sit at the kitchen table and eat the lunch her dad had fixed for her and drink milk and have cookies for dessert. She would tell them what a total disaster junior high had turned out to be. And they would say, "That's okay, Deej, we understand. If it's that bad, you can go back to sixth grade." She would be the world's oldest living sixth grader. Maybe she'd even get into the *Guinness Book of World Records.*

Again, she turned around. Enough people were still looking at her to make some sort of move necessary. She picked up the phone and dialed a number.

"Hi," she said, forcing her voice to sound chipper as the tears started to fall. "How's it going?"

The woman at the other end said in a voice every bit as cold as Mrs. Agbabian's, "At the tone the time will be twelve-thirteen and forty seconds. Beep."

FIVE

After the world's worst bus ride, D.J. arrived home where Joey, Jesse, and Danny were hanging out in the living room giving Michelle tips on how to sort her shapes. Sorting shapes. If only D.J.'s life were that simple! She clutched her books to her chest and headed upstairs hoping no one would notice her. No such luck.

"Hey, Deej!" her dad called out too cheerfully. "How did it go?"

She paused on the stairs without turning. "Oh, it was your typical first day. I got my classes and then I went to them and now I'm home. Dad, would you mind if tomorrow I dressed a little more *junior highish*?"

"No, I understand," he said. "You want to be hip. Like your rad dad."

Rad dad! When her father tried to be cool, he could be such a dweeb. Maybe dweebishness was in your genes. That's it! That would explain everything. "Eee-yeah," she said slowly. "That's it. Thanks, Dad. You're the best."

"I am good, aren't I?" he said with fake modesty.

Next, Stephanie trooped in the door. As down as her big sister had been, Stephanie was way up there.

"Second grade is so cool!" she enthused.

"Tell us about it," Danny said.

"Yeah," Uncle Jesse put in. "Give us the highlights."

"Well, you happen to be looking at the Room Seven Official Fish Feeder."

"Ooooooh," said the guys.

"And now that D.J.'s gone, when people say, 'Hey, Tanner,' I know they're talking to me."

"Way to go, Tanner!" said Joey.

"Then one of the shrimpy little first graders asks me, 'Where's the cafeteria?' I said, 'Can't you read that big sign that says CAFETERIA?' And the kid says, 'No, I can't read.' They can't even read!" She slapped herself. "What a great day!"

And off she marched upstairs to tell D.J. the good news. She was going to do just fine without her big sister.

SIX

"**According to** *Teen Beauty*," Kimmy said, studying the magazine, "we have to find our most beautiful feature and design our makeup to bring it out."

"Hmmmm." D.J. looked at her face in the mirror. "Does hair count as a beautiful feature?"

"I guess," said Kimmy. "But what about elbows?"

"Elbows?"

Kimmy showed them off. "This friend of my crazy cousin Milton once told me I had beautiful elbows."

D.J. still didn't get it. "Elbows?" she repeated.

"Maybe beautiful wasn't the word he used. I think he said expressive."

"I don't think elbows count," D.J. informed her, turning back to her own magazine.

The two girls were up with the birds this morning staging Operation Make-Over. They pooled every bit of makeup they owned, plus quite a bit of Mrs. Gibbler's. Kimmy said her mom had so much she would never miss it. Already they had skimmed at least a dozen magazines looking for tips.

But after using three kinds of blush—a gel, a powder, and a cream—Kimmy was still dissatisfied.

"Maybe I'm deformed. Maybe my cheek-bones got mixed up with my elbows accidentally."

"Just do like they say. Follow the line of your cheekbone from your nose clear out to your ear."

"I did. But I still can't see my cheekbones. Maybe if I use some of my mom's lipstick."

"That will highlight you for sure," said D.J. She was concentrating on her eye shadow. She was on her fifth color when her father called from downstairs.

"Girls! Five minutes till the bus."

"Yikes," said Kimmy. "What do you think. Are we done?"

They stood before the dresser mirror, with their hair piled up high on their heads and towels draped around their necks to protect their "hot" outfits. Kim and D.J. looked like Bozo the Clown and the Bride of Frankenstein.

D.J. applied a final layer of flavored lip gloss and smacked her lips. "Think we look old enough?"

"How old do we want to look?" Kimmy asked.

"Old enough to keep me out of that phone booth during lunch."

"At least you got to eat. I had to give my lunch to some girl with a tattoo. We could use a little more eyeliner."

Just as they were whipping out the eyeliner for the fourth time, Stephanie came in. "All right!" she exclaimed. "A makeup party! I want to look like superstar Barbie."

"Chill child," the New Improved D.J. told her. "You're way too young."

Just then, Danny called from downstairs. "Let's go, girls! It's getting late!"

"Coming, Dad!" D.J. called back. She turned to Kimmy. They took off their towels. Then they turned to Stephanie.

"Well? How do we look?" D.J. asked.

Stephanie walked around them once. "Cheap," she concluded.

"*All right!*" The friends exchanged high fives.

Down the stairs they came, with their

books held high to hide their "new looks." Just as they were hoping to slip out the door unnoticed, Danny threw himself in their path.

"Whoah!" he said

"Dad," D.J. said, lowering her books. "We have to go to school."

He smiled. "Yes, but you have to get past me first."

D.J. stamped her foot. "But you *said* I could look a little more junior highish."

"Where is this junior high? Las Vegas? You"—he pointed to Stephanie—"may go to school."

With head held high, Stephanie marched out the door. "I guess we're not as old as we thought we were."

"See you at school, Deej," Kimmy said, leaving her best friend to face her hopelessly old-fashioned father alone.

"Dad, before you say anything," D.J. began. "You were not at school yesterday. You didn't see the other girls."

"I don't care about the other girls. My

daughter is not going to school looking like Jessica Rabbit."

Joey and Jesse came in with their morning cups of coffee.

"Uncle Jesse, Joey, you're from this century. Tell him he's wrong."

They zipped their lips. They were not going to get in the middle of this one. No possible way.

"Fine, then," she said to Danny. "I'll just tie some bows in my hair, put on my Garanimals, and go skipping off to school. I'll just be Daddy's little girl forever!"

She ran upstairs in tears.

SEVEN

"Leave me alone!" D.J. called out when her father knocked on her door.

"I can't," he said, opening the door and entering. "I'm your dad. It's my job. So do you want to tell me about it?"

D.J. was sitting at the round, kid-sized table in the corner. "There's not much to tell," she said quietly. "Except that yesterday was the worst day of my life. Everyone at school looked so much older. And I was dressed exactly like this teacher everybody hates. I ate lunch in a phone booth listening to the time lady beep for twenty-five minutes and thirty seconds."

Mr. Tanner squatted onto a kid-sized chair and folded his hands neatly on the table. "I wish you'd told me this yesterday."

"I was too embarrassed. I don't know what happened. In sixth grade, I was so cool. Now I'm a joke."

"I know it feels that way," he said gently. "But that's because you were a big fish in a small pond. Now you're in a big pond, so you feel like a small fish. But you don't have to look like the big fish. Especially if the big fish are bad fish, and smelly fish, and well, now I'm lost and rambling and I just want to hug you and take you to Sea World."

"I just want people to like me," she said pitifully.

"And they will like you. As soon as they

get to know you." He turned her head to show his daughter her makeup-caked reflection in the mirror. "But this girl isn't you."

"Then who am I?"

"I guess to me, you're still my little girl. Look, I don't want to stop you from growing up. You just can't go from twelve to twenty-five overnight."

"Kathy Santoni did."

Just then Rebecca breezed in, dressed for work. "Danny, let's go. We're going to be late." Then she got a look at D.J.'s face and went pale. "D.J., don't *ever* let your father do your makeup."

"I did it myself," she said sheepishly.

Rebecca came closer and studied the full effects of the damage. "You know, when I first started wearing makeup I made the same mistakes."

"Yeah?" said Danny. "How old were you? Eighteen? Nineteen?"

"Actually, I was D.J.'s age."

"Glad I asked," he said glumly.

"Really?" asked D.J. Her spirits lifted a

fraction. "You wore makeup when you were my age?"

Rebecca nodded. "My mom taught me that the secret to makeup is to make it look as if you're not wearing any."

"How do you do that?"

"By bringing out your natural beauty. Can I show her?" she asked Danny.

"Can she?" D.J. asked eagerly.

Danny got up from the table. "I guess we can all be a little late. Go for it."

Michelle came in. She was carrying a tube of lipstick in her chubby fist. Her face was even more covered with it than Kimmy's was, if such a thing was possible.

"I look pretty," she declared.

"Yes, Miss America," her dad told her, "you look very pretty." He picked her up and held her. "But you missed Rebecca's lecture. The secret to makeup is to make it look like you're not wearing any."

Michelle scribbled lipstick all over Danny's nose.

"Daddy pretty!"

"Thanks, Michelle. I needed that."

Meanwhile Rebecca had her work cut out for her. She started by slathering cold cream all over D.J.'s face. It took an entire box of tissues to take off the makeup D.J. had loaded on. While she worked, Rebecca chatted.

"I remember my first day of junior high."

"Was it wonderful?"

"Are you kidding? It was the worst day of my life. I had gym first period. I wore this beautiful white angora sweater. Short sleeves? Pullover? Well, this tough eighth grader liked it so much she wanted me to trade my sweater for her blouse. 'Forget it,' I told her. But she got me. After gym while we were changing she grabbed my sweater and stepped on it with her dirty sneaker."

"Stepped on it!" D.J. was outraged. That sounded much nastier than what had happened to her yesterday.

"Right across the front of it. I had to go through the entire rest of the day with this huge black footprint across my chest. All

34

the boys were laughing and pointing. I thought I would die."

"That sounds pretty awful."

"But I had my good days, too. Like when the captain of the junior varsity football team invited me to the Pep Rally Dance. Close your eyes now. I'm going to do your eye shadow."

As Rebecca applied a subtle pink shadow to D.J.'s eyelids, D.J.'s thoughts drifted.

Living with her dad and Uncle Jesse and Joey was pretty terrific. Most of the time she felt lucky. It was like having three incredibly cute, really wonderful dads. Most of her friends were lucky if they had one. But sometimes—like now—she missed her mom. Her mom would have helped her over a rough spot like this one. But having Rebecca around made it seem not quite so hard.

"So what do you think?"

D.J.'s eyes fluttered open. She looked in the mirror. Her hair was full but neat, swept back from her face by two tortoiseshell combs. She had on just enough blush to make it look as if she had just come back from a walk on the beach. *Sunkissed*, just like the magazine said. Eyeliner and mascara made her eyes look larger but not harder. She looked soft. She looked natural. She looked...what could she say? She actually *liked* the looks of the girl staring back at her.

"Yes!" she cried, turning to give Rebecca a grateful hug.

"Don't thank me yet, Cinderella," Rebecca said, going to case D.J.'s closet. "Before you head out to the ball, we've got to do *something* about that dress!"

EIGHT

D.J. stepped off the lunch line and passed Mrs. Agbabian. She was so relieved! Their outfits were not alike. At all. Calmly D.J. looked around for a place to sit. Suddenly she collided with somebody.

It was Kimmy Gibbler, minus about a half a ton of makeup.

"What happened to your face?" D.J. asked.

"Oh, my mom saw me getting on the bus and freaked out. She made me wash it all off. But guess what? I got my whole schedule changed. We have the same lunch now."

"All right!"

The friends looked around for an empty table. They saw two girls sitting off by themselves.

"Hi," D.J. went over to them. "You're in my English class, right?"

"Yeah," the brunette said. "I'm Susan Erickson and this"—she pointed to her blond friend—"is Karen Sykes."

"I'm D.J. Tanner and this is my best friend, Kimmy Gibbler."

"Most people call me Gibbler," Kimmy said, grinning.

Just as they were sitting down, the snobby clique came by.

"You're sitting at our table," Colleen said.

D.J. looked up from her tray with the

friendliest of smiles. "Sure you want to sit here? It's the dweeb table now. But you're welcome to join us."

Colleen smiled poisonously. "No thanks, I'd rather eat in a phone booth."

As the clique moved off, D.J. called out, "By the way. You're wearing a little too much makeup."

The other three girls silently cheered D.J. on. She grinned at them and dug into her lunch. Maybe junior high wasn't going to be so terrible after all.

NINE

Jesse and Joey were just getting ready to do some serious worrying when Stephanie came home. She was over half an hour late. And she knew it. The usual spring was missing from her step.

"I'm home. I got kept after school. I had to sit at my desk with my head down and the lights off and I wasn't allowed to say a word for fifteen minutes. That's a new record for me. See you boys." She headed upstairs.

"Wait a second," said Jesse.

"Hold on," said Joey.

She froze at the foot of the stairs.

"Why were you kept after school, Stef?" Jesse asked.

Stephanie set down her books. She walked past them into the kitchen where she got a container of Juicy Juice out of the refrigerator. Joey and Jesse were right behind her.

"Some people were calling Walter Berman Duck Face," she finally said.

"Were you one of those people?" Jesse asked. He closed the refrigerator door for her.

"I wasn't the only one. It was the whole class." She went to sit at the kitchen table and drink her juice.

"That's no excuse." Joey sat down next to her.

"If you saw Walter, you'd call him Duck

41

Face, too. He's always making these duck lips." She swallowed a mouthful of juice and demonstrated duck lips for their benefit.

Joey said, "Kid sounds like a real quack-up to me."

"Joey." Jesse gave him a look.

"You should have seen it," Stephanie went on. "The whole class was going..." She got up and waddled across the tiles like a duck, quacking. Joey and Jesse watched, arms folded, with serious faces. "Well, Stephanie said, straightening. "I guess you had to be there."

"Stephanie," Jesse said, "let me tell you a little story about your Uncle Jesse. All the kids used to call me Zorba the Geek."

Joey slapped his knee. "Zorba the Geek!" He laughed. Jesse gave him another look. Joey stopped laughing. "Kids can be so cruel," he said earnestly.

"Uncle Jesse," Stephanie asked. "*Were* you a geek?"

"Let me put it this way. The day I turned thirteen, my whole body flipped out. My nose outgrew my face and my ears outgrew my nose. I looked like your basic Mr. Potato Head. The point is when kids teased me, it hurt my feelings. So I know how Walter feels. And I think it would be nice if you called him and apologized."

Stephanie laughed shortly. "Me? Call Duck Face?"

"Yes. You call Duck Face. I mean, eh, Walter."

"Okay, I'll call Walter and tell him I'm sorry. Then I'll invite him over for some soup and quackers." Stephanie slapped her knee. "I kill myself."

"Stephanie," Jesse warned.

"Sorry. Had to get it out of my system."

"I'll get the phone book," said Jesse. "And look up his number."

A few minutes later Stephanie took a deep breath, picked up the phone, and then hung up immediately. "Oh, too bad! I can't call Walter. D.J. is on the phone."

Joey said, "Allow me. I'll go upstairs and ask her to cut the gossip short."

43

"Oh, you don't have to do that!" Stephanie said. "That would be *too* rude."

"So is calling someone Duck Face," Jesse reminded her. "Joey. Do it."

Joey went upstairs. In a few minutes he came back down. "It took all my powers of persuasion. But the line is now clear," he announced.

"C'mon, Stef," said Jesse. "Time to make that phone call and apologize."

Stephanie opened her mouth to speak. What was this? She clutched her throat. "I can't talk," she croaked. "I lost my voice."

Jesse croaked right back at her, "Then we'll just have to go over to Walter's house and apologize in person."

"My voice is back!" she said in a normal voice. "It's amazing!"

"A real miracle," Jesse agreed. He dialed the number for her. "Trust me. You'll feel good. Walter will feel good. And I'll feel good because it was my idea. Here." He handed her the phone.

"Hello...Walter? This is Stephanie

Tanner from your class? And I'm really sorry. Well, nice talking to you." She went to hang up. Jesse blocked her.

"Don't you think you should mention what you're sorry for?"

"Oh. I'm sorry I quacked at you," she said to Walter.

Again she tried to hang up. But Jesse wouldn't let her. "And...?" he prodded her.

"And called you Duck Face," Stephanie went on. "And threw little pieces of bread at you.

"You threw bread at the kid?" Jesse asked. "Stef, he's not a real duck. You tell him he's a very nice boy."

Stephanie made a face. Her Uncle Jesse was taking this thing too far. "Walter, you're a very nice boy...you're welcome...Anything else?" she asked her uncle.

But he seemed satisfied at last. He gave her the thumbs-up sign. Relieved to be off the hook at last, Stephanie hung up. Hard.

TEN

The next afternoon Joey opened the door and found a young man standing on the doorstep. A young man in a suit and tie. And polished shoes. His hair was slicked back from his face as if he were on his way to Sunday school.

"Hi," said Joey. "Can I help you?"

"Good afternoon. Is Stephanie Tanner here?"

Joey gave a holler. "Stephanie! A friend is here."

"My name is Walter F. Berman."

Joey bit back a smile. "I'm Joseph A. Gladstone." They shook hands formally.

Danny came up behind them. "And I'm Daniel E. Tanner."

"Nice to meet you fine gentlemen," said Walter Berman.

Danny was on his way out as Stephanie came to the door. "You kids have fun. See you later, Stephanie."

For Stephanie this was not an occasion for fun.

"Walter," she said without enthusiasm.

"Hi, Stephanie."

"What are you doing here?"

Walter walked in and made himself at home on the couch as Stephanie looked on in horror.

"I just wanted to thank you in person for calling me yesterday to apologize."

"Believe me," she said, remembering how Jesse had breathed down her neck, "it was something I *had* to do."

"So you really think I'm a very nice boy?"

"Uh, yeah," she said. What else could she say?

"This is marvelous. I never thought I'd have a friend. And now I have a girlfriend."

"You do?" Stephanie asked. "Who?"

"You."

Stephanie gulped. "Me." She sat down before she fell down.

Walter put his arm around her.

"Forever?" she asked, unable to believe the fix she was in now. Thanks to her Uncle Jesse. Wait till she gave him a piece of her mind.

"Walter," she said, wriggling out from under his arm. "About this girlfriend thing."

"It's exciting, isn't it? I can't wait to tell the whole second grade that you're my girlfriend. Oh, man. I feel four feet tall!"

"Wait!" Stephanie said. "You can't tell *anyone* I'm your girlfriend."

"I get it." Walter smiled knowingly. "You want it to be a secret."

"*Top* secret," Stephanie said.

"Ooooooh! A secret girlfriend! What does that mean?" he wondered. It sounded great. Now if he could just figure out what it meant.

"Well, it means we'll never talk to each other. We'll never look at each other. We'll never hold hands. We'll be total strangers," Stephanie explained.

He looked a little uncertain. "Okay, but you're still my..."

Stephanie put her finger to her lips. "Shhhh."

"Secret girlfriend," he finished in a whisper.

She walked him to the door. "Well, I guess I *won't* talk to you later," she said, hoping he'd get the idea.

"You know what I'm doing now?" He took off his glasses.

"I'm afraid to ask," she said.

He shut his eyes tight. "I'm giving you...a secret kiss. In my mind."

Too weird. And much to her disgust, as he *thought* his kiss, he made duck lips!

As soon as he left, Stephanie shuddered. Then she went off to the kitchen to drown her sorrows in Juicy Juice.

Uncle Jesse just happened to be there, getting a snack.

"Thank you," she told him.

"What for?"

"For making me call Duck Face and apologize. Because now he thinks I'm his girlfriend. And if this gets out at school, I'm a dead duck. Have a nice day." And she took her Juicy Juice and stormed out.

"Arf," said Jesse to himself, for he knew he was in the doghouse with Stephanie now.

ELEVEN

"Kimmy, no way...with Tommy Fox? Holding hands? In the library?...No way! No way!"

D.J. was on the couch with her feet in the air and her head resting on the carpet. Uncle Jesse stood nearby, tapping his foot. He looked at his watch for the umpteenth time.

"Hurry it up, will you, Deej? We need to put in a call to a client."

D.J. covered the phone. "As soon as we finish our Spanish homework, Uncle Jesse." She went back to her conversation. "Tell me again. Where were they?"

"In the library," Jesse said. "Pay attention. We didn't have Spanish homework like that when I was in school."

Danny came downstairs. "Wrap it up, will you, Deej. You've been on for a half an hour. And I need to call the studio."

Jesse cleared his throat. "Excuse me. But someone is on line ahead of you."

"Sorry, Jesse. What has she been talking about all this time?"

D.J. covered the phone and answered, "School, Dad, what else?"

"How come every time I ask you what happens in school you say nothing?"

"What do you want to know about Tommy Fox and Kathy Santoni?"

She had him there. "Nothing," he said.

"I think I've heard enough," said Danny. "Haven't you heard enough?" he asked Jesse.

Jesse said, "I've heard more than enough."

Together they said, "D.J., get off the phone."

"In a minute, I promise," she said. Then to Kimmy, "The people in this house are so pushy."

"I'll show you pushy," her father said. "Hang up the phone. Now. There are five other people living in this house. You cannot monopolize the phone this long."

"Dad, I have the perfect solution. I should have my own private phone. Kimmy has one. So do Karen Sykes and Sue Erickson, right, Kimmy?" she said into the phone.

"A phone costs a lot of money," Danny said. "There are installation charges and—"

D.J., who had been nodding and listening to Kimmy, cut her father short. "Kimmy says it's not that expensive, Dad. To convert the extension in my room, there's a one-time cost of forty-five dollars. After that, a very reasonable monthly cost of—what was that, Kimmy?"

Kimmy told her.

"Sixteen dollars and fifty cents," D.J. relayed. "Plus nominal fees for Call Forwarding and Call Waiting."

"D.J., I don't care what Ms. Reach-Out-And-Touch-My-Wallet says. I am not just giving you your own phone," said Danny.

"I'll pay for it. I can baby-sit, just like Kimmy does. Right, Kimmy?"

Danny thought for a moment. "Well, if you can earn enough money to pay for your own phone, I'll consider giving you one."

"Great! Kimmy says I can take her job on Friday. Baby-sitting Brian Kagan. Great, Kimmy! Thanks! Bye."

At long last, to everyone's astonishment, D.J. hung up the phone.

Jesse fell upon it and dialed.

"Dad, what would we do without Kimmy?"

Danny rolled his eyes to the sky. "One can only dream."

TWELVE

"Where's Uncle Jesse?" D.J.
asked. "I'm leaving for my baby-sitting job
now and he wanted to wish me luck."

"Luck?" said Stephanie. "From him?
That would be the kiss of death."

"Stef, you're not still mad at him."

"Oh, yes, I am. Thanks to him I'll

probably be listed in *Who's Who* under D for Duck Face, Mrs. L."

"What's the L stand for?"

"Listened to her Uncle Jesse when she shouldn't have, what else?"

"Stephanie, honestly. The man's entitled to a break."

"The man's entitled to *dog food*. If I see Fido, I'll tell him you left a little early for your first day on the job. I'm baby-sitting tonight, too, for your information."

"Is that so?"

"Yeah, the guys are going to be in the basement playing cards. I'm in charge of putting Michelle to sleep. Want to see how it's done?"

Michelle was on the floor playing with her stuffed llama.

"Sure, Stef," said D.J., "I could use a few pointers."

"Okay. Michelle, it's time to go to bed."

Michelle looked up from her llama. "I'm not sleepy. See?" She bugged her eyes extra wide.

"Come on, Michelle. Let's go upstairs and play Sleeping Beauty."

"How do you play that?" Michelle asked.

"Well, you go to sleep, and that's the beauty of it."

Michelle wasn't buying it. "You sleep. I'm staying here."

D.J. grinned. "Maybe you'll have your methods perfected by the time I come home later tonight. Good luck."

D.J. walked down the block toward the Kagans' house. It was the fanciest house in the neighborhood. Jesse said the Kagans were made of money. She rang the doorbell. The chime played a weird tune. Was it an old rock-and-roll song she'd heard Jesse play?

Mrs. Kagan opened the door.

"'Sunshine of Your Love,'" she said.

"I beg your pardon?" D.J. asked.

"That's the tune of the week," said Mrs. Kagan, "on the doorbell. In case you were trying to name it."

"Oh." D.J. came in slowly. The front

hallway was very grand, but Mrs. Kagan wasn't dressed like a rich lady. She was dressed in patched blue jeans and a Grateful Dead T-shirt. D.J. wondered if she was going to a costume party tonight. But it wasn't any of D.J.'s business where Mrs. Kagan was going. It was her business to take care of Mrs. Kagan's son while she was gone. Only five more jobs like this and she would have enough money to buy her own phone. Then she would truly be a member of the Teenage Race.

Mrs. Kagan was briefing her. "We like Brian to go to bed at nine. But sometimes his inner clock says ten. So just go with the natural flow."

D.J. nodded uncertainly. Inner clock? Natural flow? Who were these people? "So, in other words, he goes to bed whenever he wants?"

"That's the rule," said Mrs. Kagan, smiling brightly. "Brian, come say hello to D.J....but only if you want to," she added.

Brian came downstairs. He wore the

cutest little pair of black karate pajamas.

"Hi, D.J.," he said. "We're gonna have a lot of fun tonight."

"That's why I'm here." She grinned up at him. *What a sweet little guy. This is going to be a snap.*

Mr. Kagan joined Mrs. Kagan. They were dressed like twins.

"Have a good time at your costume party," D.J. said as she walked them to the front door.

"Oh, we're not going to a costume party," Mrs. Kagan said, laughing. "We're going to a rock concert."

"Stay cool," said Mr. Kagan.

As soon as the Kagans were out the door, D.J. turned. Something was different about Brian Kagan. There was a light in his eyes. An evil light. She smiled at him hopefully. "Hi, Brian," she said.

"I hear it's your first time baby-sitting," he said.

"That's not really true, Brian. I baby-sit for my little sister, Michelle, all the time."

"Well," he said, his little eyes narrowing. "This will be a little different."

"Brian," D.J. said, "let's be friends, okay?"

"Gimme half the money my parents are paying you and maybe I'll be your friend."

D.J. laughed. Even though it wasn't very funny. This kid was a spoiled little monster. Kimmy had neglected to fill her in on that one small detail. *Thanks a bunch, Kimmy.* "No way, Brian. I'm saving up to buy my own phone. So, would you like to play a nice quiet game? Or would you like to go right to sleep?" Hint-hint.

Brian leapt up onto the back of the couch and assumed a karate pose. "I'm the Black Ninja Warrior Prince. And you're the Evil Lord Carnux from Dimension Zilch. Kneel before me or I'll Ninjitsu you."

He started chopping the air with his hands.

D.J. backed off, trying to stay cool. "I'm not kneeling before you, Brian."

"Wanna bet?" He grabbed a vase off the

61

coffee table. A very expensive-looking vase.
"Do what I say or I'll smash this and say
you did it."

"You wouldn't dare!"

"Oh, no?"

He threw it up in the air.

D.J. scrambled and caught it. Inches from
the floor.

"Lucky catch. This means war!"

THIRTEEN

"Brian!" **D.J.** pounded on the bathroom door. "Let me out of here this instant!"

"Not until you shave off all your hair!" Brian called back from the other side of the door. "The Evil Lord Carnux is bald. So get bald, or get flushed."

"Brian, let me out or I'll call the police."

The Kagans' master bathroom happened to feature a telephone next to the john. It also had a sunken bathtub, a towel warmer, and a furry rug. Not a bad place to be locked in...if you didn't have a job to do.

"Right," Brian said, "and tell them what?"

"I'll think of something," she replied. The kid had a point. What would she say? Help, I'm being held prisoner in the bathroom by a six-year-old. She looked at her flushed reflection in the wall-to-wall mirror. She was a wreck! This was turning out to be the longest evening of her entire life.

A little light bulb went on over D.J.'s frazzled head. It just might work. If only the Kagans had an electric razor. Sure enough, she found one in a drawer of the marble-top vanity. She plugged it in and turned it on high speed.

"Hear that, Brian?" she called through the door. "I'm doing it. I'm shaving off all my hair. Just for you!"

"You are?" he asked.

She set the buzzing razor on the counter near the sink so he would think she was in there, shaving her head.

"If you don't believe me, come in and see for yourself, Brian."

He unlocked the door. D.J. was behind it, back to the wall. When he stepped farther into the bathroom, she slipped out and ran down the stairs. Free!

"Ha! Ha! Ha!" He stood at the top of the stairs. "You may have escaped, Evil Lord. But I have your power pack."

Her purse! She had left it in the bathroom! And now Brian was going through it. "Kiss your lipstick good-bye!" he cried.

"But that's my favorite..."

Plop! Into the tropical fish tank went the tube of peach-flavored lip gloss Rebecca had given her.

Just then the doorbell rang. D.J. dived to answer it. "Kimmy!" She practically collapsed with relief. "He's got my purse!"

"Challenging assignment for a beginner, isn't it?" she asked, strolling into the house as if she owned it. "Watch a pro in action."

She went to the foot of the steps and addressed the Problem Child directly. "Hear this, Chump. Drop the purse...or I'll come up there and kiss you. On the lips."

"Yuk!" he cried, dropping the purse over the railing to the floor.

"It's not very flattering." Kimmy picked up D.J.'s purse and returned it to her. "But it happens to work."

"Thanks, Kimmy. Not that I'm complaining, but what are you doing here?"

"I just dropped by for a snack."

D.J. didn't have much of an appetite herself, what with one crisis and another. "They left me cookies in the kitchen."

"Cookies? Boring! Come on and I'll show you where they put the fancy chocolates."

FOURTEEN

They were sitting at the coffee table, washing down caramel cremes with cold milk when Brian poked his head through the banister. He was armed with a high-powered, battery-operated water machine gun.

"Prepare to die, Slime Burgers!" he cried.

In seconds the girls were drenched. They had to hide behind the couch.

"C'mon, Deej," Kimmy said. "What are we? Men or mice?"

D.J. grinned. "Don't you mean girls or gerbils?"

"Whatever? There are two of us. And only one of him."

"You're right," D.J. said firmly. Using a pillow as a shield, she rose from their hiding place. "All right, Brian. That does it. I am through playing games with you."

"You'll never catch me!" Brian shouted. He tried to pull his head out from between the rails. His water gun clattered to the floor.

"Help!" he squealed. He didn't sound so tough now. "I'm stuck!"

"Don't listen to him," Kimmy said. "He's a little faker."

D.J. had her doubts. She went halfway up the stairs. She tried to pull Brian's head out. But did not succeed. How did he get in there in the first place?

"No, Kimmy. This is no joke. He really is stuck."

"Great," Kimmy said with heartless cheer. "Let's go watch TV in peace."

Poor Brian was whimpering now.

"Kimmy," D.J. said. "You come up here and stay with him. Try to keep him calm. I'll be right back."

"Where are you going?"

"To the kitchen."

D.J. cased the cupboards. Granola. Wheat germ. She opened the refrigerator.

"Butter," she said aloud, reaching for it. One time she had gotten a ring of Michelle's stuck on her pinkie. Uncle Jesse had eased it off with butter. It was worth a try.

"I said help me," said Brian when he saw the butter in her hand, "not feed me."

"Good news, Bri. You'll be able to slide right out of there. As soon as we rub butter... all over your head."

"Oh, no, you don't!"

"You're just lucky your parents didn't have any chicken fat. I would have used that instead. Dig in, Kimmy." She offered Kimmy a handful. Grinning, Kimmy grabbed some.

"Brian, baby," Kimmy said as she started to grease his little neck. "This is going to hurt me more than it hurts you."

"Yuk! I hate this. It feels ucky!"

"Shut up and let me butter your lips," said D.J.

"Don't forget that cute little nose," Kimmy added.

"And his hair, too. Grease it up good."

"This will never work, you dumb girls."

"Watch who you're calling dumb. Banister Face," Kimmy said, stuffing some butter into his mouth.

When all the butter was on Brian, D.J. said, "I guess that should do it."

Very carefully, they both tried to ease his greasy head out. They tried this way. They tried that way. But Brian was right. Not about them being dumb. About him being stuck. He was in there for good!

D.J. bit her lip and stood back. The

Kagans would be home soon. What would they say when they saw their darling baby stuck in the railing and buttered up like a Thanksgiving turkey! There was no doubt about it: she needed help. And there was only one place to call and get it: home.

"I'm calling my dad."

"Don't do that!"

"What if Brian's neck starts to swell?"

"What if your dad won't let you baby-sit anymore? You'll never get your own phone."

"What if he starts to turn blue," D.J. said, pointing at Brian.

"Call your dad. Or," Kimmy added, rubbing her palms together, "let me go home and get my dad's chain saw."

Brian let loose with a bloodcurdling scream.

"I think I'll call my dad."

FIFTEEN

"Sorry to pull you away from your card game, Dad," D.J. greeted Danny at the Kagans' front door.

"That's okay. I was losing anyway."

"Mr. Tanner," said Kimmy, seeing the saw in his hand. "I was only joking about the saw."

"I'm afraid the saw may be the only

solution. Hi, Brian," he said. "Hang in there, guy." Now it was his turn to try and remove Brian from his fix. "This happened to my cousin Eddy one Halloween. Cousin Eddy had a big head even when he wasn't dressed up as the pumpkin ghost and stuffed with an entire pillowcase of treats. We had to saw him out. And I'm afraid, Brian, we're going to have to do the same with you."

"Be careful," the boy pleaded.

Danny set to work sawing the banister. "The butter was a nice touch, Deej. But you forgot something."

"What, Dad?"

"Parsley and a pinch of thyme. Sticking your head through these railings was a very dangerous thing to do. But we'll have you out in a jiffy. Don't move, Brian."

"Where would I go?" he asked.

"The kid has a point," said Kimmy.

"I really blew it, huh, Dad?" D.J. said. "I guess I'm not really ready for baby-sitting, or my own phone, or anything."

"It just so happens," said Danny, "I am very proud of you."

D.J. practically fell down the stairs. "You are?"

"You are?" Brian echoed.

"I am. Sometimes when you've been in trouble before, you've tried to handle the situation yourself. You ended up making things worse. But tonight, you showed good judgment. You asked for help right away. That's exactly what a good baby-sitter should do."

"Thanks, Dad." D.J. felt a little better. But not much. After all, the Kagans weren't home yet. They were bound to be furious with her. And, of course, it wouldn't occur to them to blame their own little angel. They would probably make her pay for the damage to the railing. Maybe they would even sue her. Can you be arrested for being a bad baby-sitter?

Just then she heard a car pulling into the driveway. She ran to look through the curtain. It was the Kagan's shocking pink

BMW. "Uh-oh," she said, and her heart performed flip-flops.

"Good luck," Kimmy whispered. And like the rat leaving the sinking ship, she slipped out the back door into the night.

The Kagans opened the front door. When they saw their son stuck behind bars, and their neighbor Daniel Tanner with the saw in his hand, they stopped in their tracks and stared.

"Hi," Danny smiled and waved to them with the hand not holding the saw. He looked almost casual. Like he spent every Friday night freeing small boys from banisters. "You're probably wondering what's going on."

The Kagans nodded. They didn't say a word.

"And I don't blame you," Danny went on. "As you can see, Brian got his head stuck. But I've almost got him out."

"If you're curious about the butter," D.J. said, "Well..."

Just as she was trying to figure out how

to explain what had happened, Danny sawed clean through the banister. Brian pulled out his stuck head.

"I'm free!" he cried, throwing up his arms.

"Brian, are you all right?" his father asked.

"Yes, Dad," he answered as sweet as can be. To his parents' amazement, he didn't seem at all upset.

"Thank you, Mr. Tanner. Thank you, D.J.," Brian said, like a little gentleman. Almost meekly he went off to wash the butter off his head.

Mrs. Kagan turned to D.J. D.J. started to apologize but Mrs. Kagan stopped her short. Here it comes, D.J. thought.

"We'd like to have you back on Saturday at seven," Mrs. Kagan said. "If you're available," she added.

D.J. was stunned. "I don't know," she said, looking at her father. He didn't seem to think it was the world's worst idea. And she could use the money for the phone.

"We'll double your salary," said both Kagans at once.

D.J. beamed. "See you Saturday. Seven sharp."

"A baby-sitter is born!" Danny Tanner said proudly.

SIXTEEN

Stephanie and some friends from class were in the kitchen working on their bug project for school when the terrible thing happened!

The doorbell rang and Stephanie went to answer it.

The terrible thing was waiting on her doorstep, wearing the usual suit, tie, and polished shoes. And he was carrying a big bouquet of flowers for her. Walter.

"Good afternoon, Stephanie," he said, making the famous duck lips.

"Walter," she whispered, hoping her friends hadn't heard. "This is supposed to be a secret."

He came right in the door. "That's okay," he assured her. "No one knows I'm here. Except my mom. And I told her it was strictly business. Here." He handed her the bouquet.

"Thank you." She dumped it on the table. "They're very pretty. But I have a lot of homework to do. So thank you, good night, and good luck."

She took him by the hand and pulled him toward the open door. Wouldn't you know it? Her friends picked that very moment to come out from the kitchen to see what was keeping her.

"Oooooo!" said her friend Ryan. "It's Duck Face!"

"Duck Face brought Stephanie flowers," added Harry.

"It's Mr. and Mrs. Duck Face," Laurie sniggered, pointing to the two of them, holding hands.

Realizing she was still holding Walter's hand, Stephanie dropped it quick.

But her friends were just getting warmed up.

"They're gonna get married and live in a pond," said Ryan. They all laughed.

"We're not getting married," said Walter. He was perfectly serious. "Stephanie is my secret girlfriend."

"Oh, Walter." Stephanie shook her head sadly. She stared at the floor. If only it would swallow her up!

"So, it's true," said Harry. "You *are* Mrs. Duck Face!"

The three of them started waddling around, flapping their elbows like duck wings.

"Mrs. Duck Face! Mrs. Duck Face! Mrs. Duck Face!" they chanted, over and over again. It was enough to make a person scream. Which is exactly what Stephanie did. At the top of her lungs.

"Stop it! Stop teasing me."

Uncle Jesse came downstairs to see what all the fuss was about. But he backed up when he saw it had something to do with Walter. Stephanie was still mad at him and he didn't want to risk making things worse.

"I am not his secret girlfriend," she shouted over their chanting.

They fell silent.

"I'm not his any kind of girlfriend," she went on.

"Oh, yeah?" said Ryan. "Then prove it. Call him Duck Face and kick him out."

"Yeah" said Laurie. "Do it."

"Quick," added Harry, "before we stop being your friends. Forever."

But Stephanie stood her ground. If this was how friends acted, she didn't want any part of them. "No, I'm not gonna call him Duck Face. And I'm not gonna throw him out."

"Then I guess he really is your boy-friend," said Laurie.

"No, he is not my boyfriend." She went to stand beside him. "But he *is* my friend," she added with quiet dignity.

Even Walter looked surprised. "I am? I'm your secret friend?"

"No, Walter," she explained gently. "You're my everybody-can-know friend."

She turned to the others. "And if you were really my friends, you wouldn't tease him either."

"Why not?" said Ryan. "It's fun."

"Oh, yeah? Was it fun when you got hurt during recess and everyone called you Cryin' Ryan?"

Ryan hung his head. Harry and Laurie laughed.

"I wouldn't laugh, Harry," Stephanie told him. "Remember when you got that bad haircut? Everybody called you Salad Bowl Head?"

Harry remembered all right. It was not a

happy memory. Now only Laurie was laughing.

"What's so funny?" Stephanie turned to face Laurie.

"Miss Milk Through her Nose... on Parents' Day... *Twice*."

"Hey!" Laurie said, looking wounded.

"It doesn't feel so great to be teased, does it?"

All three—plus Walter—agreed silently.

"Walter," said Stephanie, "will you stay and work on our bug project with us?"

"I'd enjoy that," Walter said. "And thanks for standing up for me."

"What can I tell you?" Stephanie said wearily. "Sometimes you just have to do the right thing. Right, gang?"

"Right," they muttered.

"Good answer," she told them. "Now, if you'll all excuse me. I have to go upstairs and see somebody about something."

SEVENTEEN

Stephanie found her uncle upstairs playing hide-and-seek with Michelle. Or trying to, at any rate.

Jesse covered his eyes. "Nine, ten...ready or not, here I come."

Jesse uncovered his eyes and looked around. Michelle popped up from behind the bed.

"Here I am!" She giggled.

"Michelle, come here. We need to talk. This is Hide-and-Seek. You are playing Hide and Say 'Here I am.' Got it?"

Michelle nodded. "Got it."

Stephanie hated to interrupt the fun. But she had something important to say. She cleared her throat. "Uncle Jesse," she said. "We need to talk, too. I mean, I have something to tell you."

"Yeah?"

"You were right. It feels terrible being teased. And I'm sorry I was so angry at you for making me apologize to Walter."

He smiled, pleased. "I may not do everything you like, Stef. And sometimes I may even make mistakes. But I'm always on your side. All I want is for you to grow up to be the best person you can be. And today, you were about as good as it can get."

Stephanie smiled. Then she looked suspicious. "How did you know?"

He shrugged. "Yeah, well, Michelle and I

were out in the hall. I was sort of listening in. And I gotta tell you. I was so proud, I nearly cheered."

She grinned. "When I grow up, I want to be just like you. But wear dresses."

He opened his arms wide. "C'mere you. For a big hug."

"Hug me, too," Michelle said.

They brought her into the hug.

After the hug, Stephanie turned and headed back downstairs. The bug project would never get done at this rate. But she paused on her way out.

"Uncle Jesse, if anyone ever calls you Zorba the Geek again, you just tell 'em to see Mrs. Duck Face."

EIGHTEEN

D. J. and Stephanie were sitting at the round table in their room doing their homework when the telephone rang.

D.J. was nearest. She picked it up. "Hello," she said.

"Hello," said her father.

"Dad! Where are you? I thought you were home."

"I am," he said, walking into the room.

87

He was speaking into the cordless phone.

D.J. stared at him. She was totally baffled. "But how can you be calling me on the same line?"

"Maybe because I called you at your own personal phone number,"

D.J. hung up the phone and screamed. "I got a phone! I got a phone!"

She leapt up and hugged her father. She jumped up and down. "Dad, I love you! You're the greatest! What's my new number?"

"555-8722," Stephanie told her.

D.J. repeated it dreamily. "I love it." Then it dawned on her. She turned to her little sister. "How'd you know my number?"

Stephanie shrugged. "Dad told me this morning and I kept it a secret all day."

"Remember our deal," Danny said. "It's your phone so long as you can pay for it. But I don't want this baby-sitting business to get in the way of your schoolwork."

D.J. was bursting with excitement. Wait till she called Sue and Karen. "No problem," she told him.

"Your own phone," Danny mused. "My little girl is growing up so fast. You know, one day that phone is going to ring and there is going to be a boy calling. And with my luck it's going to be a dentist boy or a doctor boy. And one day that boy is going to come to me and he'll say, "Mr. Tanner, you have the most wonderful, beautiful daughter in the world. You must be one heck of a dad!"

D.J. shook her head fondly. "Dad, sometimes you are so corny. But you are...one heck of a dad!"

Just then the phone rang. Her own personal phone. D.J.'s face lit up. "My first call! But who has my number?"

Stephanie nudged her aside and reached for the phone. "That will be Walter."

"But I thought you kept my number a secret."

Stephanie smiled angelically. "From you, I did."

She picked up the phone. "Hello, Walter. Yeah, you can reach me here, day or night..."

She kicked back on her bed, cradling the phone beneath her chin. As if she owned it!

For a few seconds D.J. just stared at her sister in speechless wonder. Then she turned to her father. "Do you believe this? Did you see what that little...*dweeb* just did?"

Stephanie covered the receiver. "I heard that! How rude! All I have to say is, same to you, Duck Face." And making duck lips at her big sister, Stephanie returned to her little chat with Walter.

"Remind me," D.J. told her father. "To get a lock for my phone."

"Or a zipper for the duck lips," her father agreed.

All three of them started quacking at once. Great minds worked the same way when they were all part of the same full house.